BEDTIME STORIES

PACKAGE INSERT

Composition

This book consists of three parts:

"The Puppet's Journey to Bolzano" Students sometimes like to take a semester abroad, and Susanne is no exception. But her journey on foot to Italy is interrupted when she gets lost. And yet finds something in the process ...

"House Sitter" Shannon has been working as a house sitter for a long time to finance her studies. But this time, nothing goes as she is used to. Quite the opposite ...

"Green is not your color" As an analyst and broker in New York City, Adele earns a lot of money, but also has her own peculiarities. Which she also lives out again and again - always with someone else. But this time, it will probably be forever ...

Presentation For reading with the eyes.

Fields of application Content as a sleep aid in cases of still insufficient tiredness.

Contraindications Keep away from children and minors under eighteen (18) years of age!

Side effects Paperback formats and Kindle® devices, or other suitable eBook readers, may fall on your nose in case of sudden onset of sleep, and insufficient distance from the face.

Interactions Do not read with other books at the same time, it will only cause confusion. Do not combine with alcohol, becauz te helf of tha kontend iss misin thann.

Dosage instructions Read each story individually, lying flat or with the upper body slightly elevated in bed.

Method and duration of use Read one story each day directly before going to sleep. Repeat as often as you like.

The Puppet's Journey to Bolzano

I had been on the road for almost a month, putting one foot in front of the other every day. In between, of course, I had already thought of giving up; after all, I could also have taken the train. But that wasn't the point: the journey was the goal! Over three-hundred fifty miles on my feet from my hometown to the university in Bolzano. How crazy could I be? But I never regretted it in the meantime. Okay, fine. Maybe once or twice. But not all together. Because, without this trip, I wouldn't have seen or experienced many things. The accident on the highway, when I was running alongside. The birth of the calf right next to my tent, in the middle of the night. The many nice people I was allowed to spend the night with - without them asking me anything for it. Well, sometimes they didn't know that I was lying in their barn, snoring. But still, I would never forget this trip. Of that I was sure. What I couldn't be sure of right now was the way ahead. I had a map, and knew how to use it; but somehow, I had gotten lost in the last half hour. According to the map, the path should have led me into a valley. Instead, it went uphill. Only slightly, but steadily. This wasn't supposed to be. At least I didn't seem to be the only person in the area; because, on the road, which was now approaching me from the left, there were clearly traces of a tractor with a trailer. It had stopped raining only an hour ago, the water was still standing in the imprints. I looked at them more closely to find out if, and when, in which direction I should follow them. Yes, I know: I think you can use a map? Sure I can! But sometimes it's just better to ask for directions than to run wild. Period. So, which way? The tracks went both ways, uphill and downhill. But the trailer seemed to be full downhill, the tracks were noticeably deeper, and a bit out of place. So, along there. Fortunately, tractor tires always had that arrow-like tread, so I knew which lane went up, and which went down. I followed the road, always nicely along the slope. It now became stonier again, but interspersed with chunks of tarmac. Probably left over from road construction somewhere, and dumped here. I made progress, even though the way set me back quite a bit. From the peaks I could see, it was obvious that I must have already deviated more than a mile from my originally planned route. But that didn't bother me, quite the opposite. I would enjoy human company after three days of solitude in the tent quite well. And I would have that, because to my right, a fence appeared. Okay, a little shaky and weathered. But a fence. Then, my steps automatically lengthened as the scent of freshly cut grass hit my nose. It couldn't be far now. But now the path rose again, significantly. I stopped, took a breath, and was that a bell? Quietly, but clearly. Such a one from sheet metal, how one ties them to animals. Already I ran off, always after the clattering, further up the road. And down again? The fence disappeared, the meadow too. Damn. The tinny tinkling was also gone. All right, let's look around again, and then decide. Single, stunted trees below, scree and meadow above. Forest below, rock above. The decision was not difficult: forest, of course. So, I went on. One foot in front of the other. The path made a bend, it went into the forest. I looked back again, down here it looked much more peaceful than where I had come from. After a while, the trees became light again, again there was a fence. But more neat, not so much weathered. Relieved, I walked on, a group of smaller trees still on the left side of the slope, and then the path would continue down the hill. Again, a fence, but this time with a gate. And a tractor behind it. A hut. Smoke from the chimney. There had to be someone here I could ask. I stopped, looked, and there really was someone standing there. Okay, an old woman. Gray skirt, tattered jacket, rubber boots, headscarf. Standing there in front of the pathetic looking hut, petting a goat with her back to me. Anyway, it was worth a try: "Bonschorno! Hello Senyora! Puee ayutare me, per favore? Sto zercanto un modo peer racconshare la prottzimmah Cheetah?" Yes, admittedly my Italian was quite bumpy. Or rather, it was really bad. But I got a reaction, the woman faltered in her action. She nudged the goat, "Andiamo! Vai!" Grumbling in protest, the goat went away, then the old woman turned around and my eyes opened a little. Well, basically I don't believe in God. But if He is responsible for something like this, then maybe I should think about it again. Because that, what stood there in only a few feet opposite me, was not an old woman at all. That was a damn pretty girl! Even about my age, with flowing, fiery red hair. She had taken off her headscarf, and was looking at me as if I was dumb. That's just how I felt as

I tried to repeat my question, "Um, cwesto parcorso con-doushe a una cheetah?" "Sometime, yes," I got the answer with a slight grin, relieved now I still wanted to know, "Ah, good! Cvando e lonntanno dal ..." Instantly my face fell in on itself. Had she just spoken English to me!? My arm pointing along the path sank down with my shoulders. My counterpart had to firmly press her lips together to keep her from laughing out loud. "My Italian sucks, doesn't it?", I asked quietly and quite bluntly, the girl nodded, "Yes. Very much so. It's nice that you tried at least, though." "Hmm, thanks," I grumbled, then remembered my question, "Oh, uh, will I get to a village or town if I keep walking along here?" "Like I said; eventually, you will," the girl said, "but you won't make it today. It's sure to start raining in the next hour, and besides, it'll be dark soon. It's still a good eight miles." I realized that was really too far. "Can I maybe pitch my tent here?", I wanted to know instead, "Would be for one night only. And I'm not making a fire." "It's too steep for a tent," the girl said, coming over to the fence, "It won't work. You're welcome to stay here in the hut for the night, though." She took off the rope that held the gate shut, opened it, and stretched out her hand to me, "Adelia, hello." Stunned by this beautiful name which really suited her perfectly I took her hand and went inside, "Susanne." "So, where are you from?", Adelia wanted to know, I told her, "From Germany." "You say?" "Thuringia." "Okay?" "Weimar." "I've heard that before." "Buchenwald?" "Ah!" came immediately, because everyone knew that. It was also easier to tell that as a tourist than to mention Goethe or Schiller. Not everyone has proper education. "Do you still grill people there?" grinned Adelia, I gave her the appropriate answer: "No, nonsense! We'll banish them to the galleys with the Romans by now." "That hit home," Adelia smiled at me. I melted away, and walked after her to the entrance of the hut like a little dog. "Well, come on in… are you okay?" "What?", I asked, completely snapped out of my reverie, "Oh, yeah. Yeah, it's all good. No problem at all. Thanks." With one eyebrow raised, Adelia followed me inside, I was amazed at first, "Wow! It's bigger than it seems from the outside." "Yes, it is," my hostess said, ushering me in, "There's the toilet and shower in the back, there's the bedroom, and right here behind the door, the kitchen. Well, it's a gas stove. Feel free to put your backpack down, and make yourself at home." I did, while I continued to look around, my hostess hung her jacket on a hook behind the door. The cabin looked old and weathered from the outside; but in here, it was like new. Two cabinets of a kitchenette with a small refrigerator, a table big enough for six people. "Are you hungry?" Adelia wanted to know; I nodded, "Yes, I am. Don't bother, though. I've got everything with me." "Yeah?", to me was smiled at nicely, and I had a pot held under my nose, "Anything this good too?" "No, definitely not," me and my tummy muttered together, Adelia grinned knowingly and placed the pot on the gas stove, "Are casunziei from grandma, the beets are a bit overcooked, though." "It doesn't matter at all," I waved it off, "I haven't had anything this tasty in ages." Adelia moved her lips, but said nothing. I noticed, but didn't measure it with any importance because of my hunger, and the pasta smelling insanely delicious; even cold. "Is there anything I can do to give you a hand?", I inquired politely. Adelia slumped for a blink, then said, "Uh, yeah. There are plates, and silverware down there." She tapped her foot on the kitchen cabinet next to her, I opened it, and took out what we would need. Then, I noticed my terribly dirty hands in contrast to the white plates, "I should probably wash my hands first." "Yeah sure, back there," Adelia pointed to me with her head, "it's just cold water." "No problem," I said, "will be fine." Once in the room with the toilet, I washed my hands with the really ice-cold water, shook and dried them. The room was not very large, but still tastefully decorated. Any self-respecting department store could take a leaf out of this decor and furnishings. Back in the living room, the decoration here also caught my eye positively. Not so alpine as it would have been expected. No, rather womanly elegant. A little too womanly. Admittedly not for my taste, I would be proud of such a decoration in my poor dorm room. Adelia obviously noticed my admiration, "Do you like it?" "Oh yes, very much so," I admitted bluntly, "could be mine. Decorated it yourself?" "Yes, it's my retreat from the city," she explained, "it's always noisy and hectic and stuff. Not here with my grandparents. I come here every summer." "I'd like that too," I agreed, "it's nice and quiet and secluded." "Except when a tourist gets lost here for the semester break," I was smiled at, and I couldn't believe it, "You study!? What, and where?" "Agricultural economics in Bolzano. Why?" asked Adelia. "That's where I want to go!", I exclaimed joyfully, "Well, for design. But I don't believe that now." "Yeah, I can't believe it either," came very joyfully from Adelia, "how long do you want to stay?" "Well, actually just for the winter semester," I said, "but who knows what's to come." Adelia rattled the pot on the stove, and I finished setting the table, adding two bottles of Fanta from my backpack. My hostess grinned when she saw it, *"Sul serio?"* "What do you mean?", I asked, Adelia returned nice and neat: *"Fanta è la Germania, ma qui è l'Italia. Cosa bevi qui, eh?"* I thought for a moment, then, *"Vino?"* *"Allora, bene.* It's there behind you in the cupboard, glasses too." I had to smile as I pulled out the bottle, because it was so typically bulbous, and wrapped in straw at the bottom. "Made it yourself?", I wanted to know, because there was no label on it. "No, just decanted," Adelia announced, "It's actually adulterated booze from a carton. Looks silly on the table, though, so better that way." I took a sip in one of the glasses and tasted, "Oh well. I've drunk worse. The main thing is that it spins." "It does what?" asked Adelia, putting the now hot casunziei on the plates. I explained to her, "When you're drunk, it does make everything spin. And the more alcohol, the more revolving it is." *"Ha senso, eh,"* Adelia made and put the pot away again, *"mangia ora, altrimenti si raffredderà e poi non avrà più un buon sapore. Buon appetito!"* "Thank you," I returned, "smells really delicious." *"Grazie a nonna, non a me. Non sarei in grado di cucinare questo,"* Adelia spoke, I had to think for a moment. Then I had understood her sentence, "You can't cook?" "I would even scorch a pot of only water," Adelia apologized with a shrug, I knew the problem, "I'm no different. At home we often have stuff from a can." "At my place, too. Only here it's Italian cans," Adelia grinned. I had to laugh, then I said, "I guess it all comes from the same factory. Only the label is different." "Yeah, one could almost think so," Adelia confirmed, then wanted to know something completely different: "What fascinates you about design? It's not fashion, I hope?" "No," I bragged, chewing, "fashion is terrible. Functionality is more important than looking good. But if you can combine the two, just like here with the bench below me. Practical, comfortable, and also functional. That's what makes good design, I think." Adelia took a quick look under the table, and shook her head, "It's a bench. Can you go wrong with that?" "Well, not really, basically," I admitted, "but what if you could make it into a bed, for example? With a bedside lamp and an adjustable headboard, and it still looks like a bench." "A bed, huh? In the kitchen?", Adelia smiled at me, "For what? Too many spins?" "Why not?", I returned, "Especially here in the cabin. If one day your grandparents come here or something?" *"Dio,* I can't have them here!" groaned Adelia. I wondered, "Don't they cook for you?" "Yes, they do. And pretty well, as you've already admitted yourself. But this is my kingdom up here, all by myself. Ever since I was fourteen." "What happened?", I wanted to know, Adelia just said, "Nothing at all? Here, fill this up!" She held her glass out to me, and I poured. I didn't want to ask any more questions; it was none of my business. So, I poured myself a glass and drank it up: "Wow, not bad at all." "Well then it's a good thing there's more of it," Adelia laughed, "because the way you're drinking, the bottle won't last long." "Well thank you too," I grinned, and immediately poured more. Adelia was grinning now too, emptying her glass and then the bottle inside. "You're not going to drink me to the floor now, are you?", I inquired as she retrieved a new bottle from the cabinet. Adelia looked deep into my eyes and smiled at me, "I don't think that's going to happen. I've only got two bottles." Immediately, I felt richly warm. I could rule out the possibility that it was the wine. Firstly, I was used to alcohol, secondly, the wine really wasn't the best, to be honest, and thirdly, I already knew such a deep look. Which was, in a way, already several times to my disadvantage. Because, I have never hidden that I can do purely nothing with men. This time, however, it didn't seem to be a disadvantage, because Adelia's face, or rather the part of her face that lay between her eyes and nose, clearly changed color when I returned her gaze. "Is there a particular reason why you prefer to be up here alone?", I wanted to know in a very warm voice, without averting my gaze for even a fraction of a second. Adelia had to swallow, then she reached for my glass, and emptied it without setting it down. She wiped her mouth, put the glass back, and just nodded silently. Whatever was outside suddenly didn't interest me anymore. The world was just happening here in this hut. Only at this table. Only between Adelia and me. I pushed the still steaming plate gently away from me, I didn't care about the food now. I was hungry, of course, but the other hunger was just getting the upper hand. "We...we should...the food...," Adelia stammered, but even she didn't avoid my gaze. Using my feet, I pushed back along with the chair, then the table followed to the left. Adelia's breath deepened considerably, but so did mine. "I should probably take a shower first or so," Adelia said in a whisper, putting her index finger in her mouth, then wiping her cheek. Clearly, a lighter mark remained. "Yeah, I guess so," I said smiling sagely, "I've been out all day, too." She was barely two feet away from me, but it seemed like a thousand light years to me. Way too far. So, I stood up, and Adelia followed my every move. Not only with her eyes, but she rose as well. A small step I took towards her, she came towards me. I could almost feel her breathing, so another tiny step. Again, Adelia came towards me, now we were not a hand's width apart. "Only gives cold water though," she breathed to me, my right hand finding her hip. "When it reaches the bottom, it will boil," was my answer, and I could barely contain myself. Adelia probably didn't feel any different, because she said, "I guess it won't even reach the bottom." In my stomach, everything started to hum;

a whole army of butterflies just set their wings in motion. With trembling fingers, I untied the knot in the gray rope that held her skirt over her hips, her hands undid my belt. Already her dress fell to the floor, from mine I had to free myself with a few small movements of my hips. But then, those trousers lay on the floorboards, too. What was leading me to Adelia's blouse. Her fingers were already busy with the hem of my shirt when I ran my hands under her blouse, and without looking, lifted it over her bosom. Forced to let me go now, already my shirt had disappeared somewhere, and I could continue to devote myself to Adelia's clothes. Almost fearfully, Adelia let me lift the blouse over her head, as naturally and probably hoped for by her, my hands grazed the piece from her arms, but kept their place high above our heads. She obviously did not want to resist the now following but still cautious kiss, because preventing me from doing so seemed to make no sense to her. The next one I gave her less carefully, the third one she gave herself, finally letting her arms sink down to mine. Demanding, she almost devoured me, but I had no concerns that this could happen. Her hands searched my back and found, only seconds later my bra fell to the floor and I was freed from all constraints. For shoes and socks, I had already taken care of myself during the kissing. However, there were still two, no, four pieces of clothing left. Because, that Adelia wore stockings I saw only now. They had to go, of course. So, I pushed Adelia with my body the two steps back to the chair, let her sit down, and put her left leg on my shoulder. With a look that made it unmistakably clear that I was way too slow, Adelia watched me roll her stocking down from above her knee to above her toes. The left leg followed in the same way, now Adelia grabbed my butt and freed me from my panties. As soon as my feet carried me again after slipping out, Adelia's nose crawled up me, from my knee to my neck. But she was also still in her panties, so I put both hands inside at her hips and freed what was underneath. Now it was my fingertips working their way up from Adelia's feet to her neck. I couldn't keep my eyes closed on the way up, of course, and noticed that Adelia was wearing a flowing mane of hair, but not just on her head. Once back at eye level, Adelia demanded another kiss, then I took her by the hand and pulled her into the shower stall. The still ice-cold water didn't deter me, but I turned the faucet on just enough for the water to drip out of the showerhead. I let the brown natural sponge run full, squeezed it out and put a little of the strawberry shower gel on it. To me, it was clearly noticeable that Adelia was a little afraid of the touching of the sponge. But I distracted her with a kiss, and I was already running it down her back. What led to the fact that she bent it, and pressed herself with the belly firmly against me. This did not remain with me without consequences, but I was not yet ready. First it was necessary to get rid of everything that the outside world had accused us of during the day. I soaped every centimeter of Adelia's body, leaving out only one certain spot by purpose. Adelia finished soaping that spot, then she rinsed out the sponge, and it was my turn to soap. Adelia also left out my spot, I took the sponge from her, and did it myself. But only to find that Adelia was already on the verge of following my movements with the sponge on herself. Of course, I couldn't let that happen, so I opened the faucet fully, and cooled Adelia down a bit. Rinsing her off in the process was rather incidental. But Adelia did not let this small meanness sit on itself of course. Involuntarily I did not leave the shower head to her, but I had not counted on the following icy cold. Clearly, the water was already initially very cold. But that now no ice cubes instead of water drops came out, surprised me. I wouldn't call it goose bumps which distributed itself over my body anymore, those were the Himalayas. Adelia then also had a sense of cold, turned off the water, handed me the towel that was hanging on the wall outside next to the shower cubicle, and whispered in my ear on the way out, "I'll make us a little warm, okay?" I couldn't really answer her, my teeth were clattering too much. I quickly stepped outside as well, and dried off. Actually already finished, but still covered all over with heavy goose bumps, the towel then remained stuck where it was during the last drying. Because looking up, I noticed Adelia. She was standing bent over in front of the small stove in the living room, adding wood neatly. But since she had not crouched down, but was bent over pushing the logs into the stove hole, I was presented with a sight that made me instantly forget all about the cold. Adelia's skin was almost white and incredibly delicate, her physique now very feminine, and a narrow gap remained between her legs, revealing the most beautiful part of her body. She stood just two steps away from me. I would have loved to fall to my knees and slide to her, sinking my head between her buttocks. But Adelia just stood back up, closed the oven door, and then turned to me. She looked at me, noticing me and my towel. But also, that the cloth had gotten caught between my legs as if by accident, and that I was obviously having trouble getting it out of there. In any case, my teeth biting into my lower lip could well have been interpreted that way. My gaze wandered from her feet over her knees, further up to her belly button, over her neck and directly into her light green eyes. Slowly, very slowly, she pulled the towel she had just fastened back off her head. I retrieved mine from where it was just stuck. The sun, in a final struggle against the falling dusk, sent a red-gold ray directly into Adelia's midsection. Her thin, almost like cotton candy looking pubic hair flashed warmly, and sparkled like a thousand diamonds. Due to the intense lighting, nothing remained hidden from me now, it was a simply indescribable, wonderful sight. I stretched out my hands to her, with the left fingertips I just reached her hip, Adelia came a step closer. Now my right fingers became entangled in the rampant fur between her legs. My left hand reached around Adelia's waist, and pulled her closer. Her arms reached my shoulders, gently pushing me backward into the room with the bed. Playing and kissing, I allowed myself to be pushed until, stimulated by the edge of the bed, I came to sit half on the bedspread and sheets. Adelia placed her knees between mine on the bedspread. My thighs opened automatically, my heels found Adelia's soles and gave her support after she lay on top of me, bracing herself on the blanket while putting me in the right position. Her hands gave up their support function, pushing my knees onto the mattress. We kissed tenderly, my nibbling teeth on her lower lip goading us both. Slowly, Adelia began to gyrate her hips, I was following her play in the opposite direction as best I could. My nipples became spear points, hers responding immediately. Adelia's movements became brisker, her breathing faster, I used my free hands and pressed her butt down on me to her rhythm. Neither of us had closed our eyes for a second, and I felt as if every blink was one too much. With every breath I absorbed both of our desires into me, with every kiss, every flick of the tongue I scaled unimagined heights. Then, when the tiniest droplets of sweat formed on Adelia's nose, and I myself was on the verge of forgetting everything around us, her eyes widened and she stopped. She pushed herself up from the bed with her forearms, I tried to keep her with me. But now sitting on me, she begged my arms to let her go. *"Aspetta ... aspetta,"* she literally begged me, "I have to tell you something first." With a worried look, I asked, "What is it?" "Nothing," came back, "it's just ... I'm a little embarrassed." I had no idea what Adelia was trying to tell me so sheepishly. But then she said it, blushing bright red because of "Well, I … I always leak like hell when … you know." Without much movement, I quickly twisted my legs under her, slid down a bit, then abruptly took my knees and hands and brought her over my breasts very close to my head. "So be it," I said, unimpressed, and sank my mouth into her lap before Adelia could even give me an answer. Her hands slapped in front of her mouth, and a powerful moan escaped from behind it as my lips reached hers. I sucked and kissed, running my tongue firmly over everything I could find. Adelia still tried to escape me, but my arms wrapped around her waist and prevented her from doing so. Unspeakably, she suffered sweet agonies. Then, her womb became heavier, she began to pant, and then pushed herself up from me with force! Even with her lips pressed together she screamed uncontrollably, reared up, and exposed to me what she was afraid of: with violent contractions, she ejected clear gushes that came off slightly sticky, and dripped hotly on my neck. I watched in fascination as Adelia's release left her, but then noticed the fearful, almost frightened look she gave me, still pulsing with short breaths. With a reassuring look, I closed my eyes briefly, then my arms pulled her lap back over my mouth. With soft, gentle movements, I took in everything that was still there without taking my eyes off Adelia. Initially irritated, but then understanding that there was nothing to be ashamed of, she enjoyed my play, and even pressed a little more with her eyes closed in devotion. Finally, she smiled, lifted herself off me, and slid down a little. I carefully wiped my neck and chin clean with the tip of the pillowcase, then embraced Adelia, and pressed her tightly against me. Which she reciprocated, then wrapped half the comforter we weren't lying on over us, and puffed contentedly. So did I, but then Adelia's head suddenly snapped up a bit, "Lie just like that." She spoke it, and slid under the covers. I did nothing and waited, Adelia flopped down on me and out of bed, but stayed under the covers. She didn't left the bed, though. Not all the way, anyway. Her feet and knees probably hit the floor; I could hear that. But the rest of her body remained covered. I lifted my head to see what she was doing. I didn't recognize anything, but probably noticed her hands under my knees. Before I could ask or react in any other way, Adelia pulled me to her with a proper jerk. Protest did not occur to me. The covers swung back and I saw and felt Adelia's hand pressing firmly into my middle. Pleased, I took a deep breath. My thighs were widened, and my legs were placed on her shoulders. Then Adelia started with a play that I would not have expected in any case. Wide and deep her hands claimed my pelvis, I could hardly breathe. Surrendering to her hands, I dived loudly into a world that I had never experienced before. The soft bed under me only added to Adelia's demands on me, I swung simultaneously in all possible directions. Then, all of a sudden and completely unexpectedly, Adelia placed a finger, moistened with my own, one floor below. She pressed it against her hand inside me, I opened my eyes and mouth wide and exploded! A green-yellow aura enveloped me, my own screaming sounded like music in my ears, and I shook to such an extent that I could not have imagined even in my wildest dreams. For seconds, I could not grasp a clear thought, everything surrounding me had moved into the far distance, and I myself consisted only of a wonderful feeling of unspeakable bliss. Then, the world around me came back, much later it should not have been. I struggled for breath, feeling Adelia leaving my midst, and lie down on me. Still barely comprehending what had just happened, I tried to hug her. But I was far too busy experiencing the convulsions still coursing through me to be able to do so. She kissed my head and shoulders, pulling the covers over us. Her legs wrapped around me, her arms held mine tightly, her hips came to rest on mine, and barely placed, her mound of Venus was already rubbing over mine. I was not yet completely back from one world, already I plunged into the next! Adelia's breasts pressed on mine, her nipples stabbed and I took off again. Not an inch I could move, and only breathe through Adelia's still slightly strawberry-scented hairs. Her pubic hair scratched only very slightly with every movement, but they did so in exactly the right place. Incited by the inability to move and Adelia's deeper and more violent breathing, I continued to climb. Something held me back, however, though I could not make out what.

24

Only when Adelia reared up slightly, panting heavily, and a hot gush poured over my middle, was that the hitherto missing trigger, and I burst like an overfilled balloon! Again and again, both of us spasmed together until Adelia finally gave up and just collapsed on top of me, limp but panting happily. I lost all control too, but Adelia was so well on top of me that she didn't fall off. Warm, soft, exhausted, content, and happy, I just closed my eyes and fell asleep.

I woke up again because a door squeaked. With my eyes still closed, I noticed the new day. Adelia was probably no longer in bed, but her leaving could not have been long ago: My back was still much too warm. Yesterday came up inside me, a wonderful shiver of memories slowly creeping up from my womb across my stomach. I knew I couldn't harbor this feeling for long, so I snuggled up tight once again and just enjoyed it. Again, the door squeaked, metallic rattling sounded softly, and water ran. Then footsteps came closer, I began to smile. Adelia sat down on the edge of the bed, and stroked my hair tenderly, *"Buongiorno tesoro."* *"Buongiorno,"* I returned very sweetly and reached out my hands to her. Adelia, however, just sighed and said sadly, *"Come vorrei, coniglietto.* But it's almost noon, and still so much to do." Immediately my face contorted into a single pout, but Adelia didn't respond, *"Non hai scelta tesoro, deve alzarti adesso. Vai."* She tousled my hair, then stood back up, and left the little cubbyhole where the bed was. Had she simply checked off yesterday? Slightly grumpy, I rose anyway, but still with some hope. And I was not disappointed. Arrived in the living room, Adelia was already waiting for me with water warmed on the stove, three towels lying on top of each other on the floor, the sponge in her hand, and a broad grin. With a half-crestfallen and half-joyful face, I approached her in lucky anticipation. But when I tried to reach for the sponge, she withheld it from me, "Out of question." Immediately I understood why the towels were there on the floor and blushed immediately, "I … you …" "Yes," Adelia simply said softly, pushing me back a step with her index finger. My toes dug into the towels still slightly damp from yesterday, everything started dancing in my head. Caring, Adelia checked the water, then dipped the sponge in, squeezing it just slightly. Catching the falling drops with her left hand, she came to me and said tenderly, *"Chiudi gli occhi."* I think she could tell I was thinking for a moment, so she repeated her request, "Close your eyes." I had never been washed by another human being before. Let alone had I even allowed that to happen. After all, I wasn't an old woman! But with Adelia, it was somehow different. Full of anticipation, quivering, I even longed for it. Regularly greedily I expected her touches, and could not explain it to myself. Already last night, after the uneaten meal, I had neither fear nor shame. Nor afterwards, when Adelia did with her hands what had never been done to me before. Even more so when she restricted my movement so much that all I had left was to breathe. And now, expecting her touch at any moment, neither. In the few split seconds it took Adelia to carry the sponge from the bowl to me, every fiber of my body literally cried out in rapture. Already the sponge was grazing my shoulder, and I began to shiver. The water was warm, Adelia was gentle and tender. I kept my eyes closed while Adelia freed me from the traces of last night. Bravely, I lifted my arms and legs when she wanted me to. I enjoyed each of her touches, each wipe and stroke. Then, after a little eternity, I guess I was clean enough. Adelia gave me a kiss; I opened my eyes and was now still dried. And even now I enjoyed the rubbing, wrapping and wiping. Every hidden part of me was treated with care by Adelia, every little bit of water was removed. Finally, I was examined, found clean and dry, and was allowed to get dressed. Finished with that, I stood next to the stove again, Adelia gave me my jacket and my backpack: "Here, you wanderer, get going. I have packed something for you, water and also something to eat. It's not far to the village, you should easily be there by evening. So, before the weather gets worse again. Guido's will have a room for you, and when you've had breakfast, you can take the bus to Durnholz. There's one leaving for Bolzano at noon, and you can sign up there." "Will I see you again?", I wanted to know hopefully, Adelia helped me with the backpack and gave me a slap on the butt, "God have mercy on you if not. Now get going. And don't turn around!" She gave me another kiss, then pushed me towards the door. I wanted more, but Adelia didn't give in, "Go, I'll see you when you get to Bolzano." Her arm pointed to the gate, her face said the same, and so I went. Whistling happily to myself, I skipped off.

Adelia was right, the way was not far. After barely two hours, I could already see the steeple of the village. But my stomach now made it clear that I was hungry. A little off the path stood a tree stump, I climbed up the short slope, and sat down. Adelia had packed me food, after all, and water to go with it. I took the bottle out of my backpack and took a sip, then I unpacked the sandwiches she made, and had breakfast. I had just swallowed the first bite when I froze. What the heck was I doing here!? Leaving the house without breakfast? Just doing what I was told to do? Taking the bus, even though I had decided to walk the whole way? But all this did not look like me at all. The day before yesterday I would not have done that. Not for the life of me! Today, however, I sat here at the wayside, and bit like a schoolgirl into her lunch. Why!? I could just go. Remembering Adelia as a nice detour, and keep walking. Very deep down, though, I knew she wasn't only a detour. Overnight, Adelia had become the person I would put my life into their hands. Had to put. With joy. Startled, my hand sank down with the bread in it. Had I really thought that just now? I would put my life into her hands with joy? Doubting myself, a thought came to me that I hardly understood. For the answer to the question, addressed to myself, was yes. A definite yes. Every cell in my body nodded in agreement and I realized that this must be the truth. I relived, just to be sure, the last few hours in my mind. The shower that evening, freezing cold and yet so warm. Adelia's hands, how she carefully soaped me. How she tampered with the stove, and pulled the towel out from between my legs. Lying on me, sitting on me, as her hot flood ran down my neck. Her hands burying themselves in me. The tight embrace that left me barely breathing. The morning wash that I had so enjoyed. Even when she pushed me out the door, I wanted it. I wanted it! Adelia wasn't the first girl I'd slept with. I'd also had relationships before. But they all didn't last very long. I was always missing something that I never knew what it was. Now I do: I wanted to be needed. But not in the way that I took care of someone else. No. I was supposed to be the one being taken care of. I was to be the one to be used. Like a machine that was turned on and off. A doll, a toy, a thing existing only for this one purpose. I took another bite of the bread, wanting to figure out what it meant. Another sip from the bottle, only now did I see it. Down, painted on the bottom of the bottle, was her name in mirror writing. I knew immediately why she had written it there. In exactly this way. It was her bottle, her property. And so was me. Immediately, I rewrapped the rest of the food, put the bottle back in the backpack, and looked up at the sky. As Adelia had announced, there were dark clouds, it was already drizzling unnoticed by me. I must have sat here for quite a long time, because dusk was already falling. But I could not possibly go to the village. I had to go back. To Adelia. To my owner. Stumbling, I ran, knowing I would be soaked to the bone, and arrive only in complete darkness. But that didn't bother me, I couldn't let it bother me. I had run away from her. A lonely pet, lost in the middle of the wilderness. A few times I stumbled, a few times I fell down. But that didn't stop me. It took me barely half the time to get back that it had taken me to run away. Finally arrived, I stepped through the gate, went inside the dark hut. After closing the door again behind me, I simply dropped my backpack to the floor. Excited, but quietly, I crept to the bed. But it was empty. The stove was hot, though, and smoke had also reached my nose when I arrived at the gate. Indecisive, I stopped for a moment, when the typical sound of a lighter sounded behind me. A warm shine, first brighter and then immediately darker, appeared. I turned around, and went into the living room. Adelia was sitting on the bench, as if she had been expecting me, and knew exactly why I had returned. Scowling, she looked at me, "Didn't I send you away?" I nodded and stammered, "Yes, had ... but I can ... I'm ..." "Do I have to take you by the hand, and walk you there?", I was asked, this time I just nodded. Adelia stood up with a sigh, and came over to me, "My goodness. You're soaked to the bone. And you're dirty." Shaking her head slightly, she circled me. Stopped inches away from me, arms crossed in front of her chest, "Well. I guess there's only one thing left to do, huh?" A brief pause followed, then Adelia ordered, "Strip." I nodded again, and dutifully removed my jacket as Adelia demanded to know, "What do you think you're doing?" I paused, already with my hands on the hem of my T-shirt. Adelia leaned forward a little, and whispered in my ear with a smile, "That wasn't meant for you."

House Sitter

I guess I'll never be done with that anyway," I sighed, pushing myself away from the desk while sitting on the chair, "but at least now you can be alone for a whole week." "You're going to be alone with your job, though, aren't you?" my suitcase-packing roommate asked. Alice, we've been sharing a room at Central State in the Quad for a year. I'm from Oklahoma here, she's not. A move-in girl, they'd say in my town. Because Alice is from Puerto Rico. Well, not really. Her mother used to buy the fresh vegetables at the market, and bring them to the military base. Her father was one of the chefs there. One thing led to another, and then Alice came along. Here on campus, we are always mistaken for twins. Although I can't say we're alike. She's a Marvel kid, I love DC. Alice goes to McDonald's, I prefer the King; Alice Pepsi, Shannon Coke. That's me, by the way. So, Shannon. And thanks for the sympathy. I would have loved my parents had picked a different name, too. Still, we look insanely alike: brown semi-long hair, small round face, barely any neck, narrow shoulders, flat chests, mini-belly, hips plus ass with warning beacons right and left - and then there are two tree trunks for legs. All in all, we're not ugly, but we're not likely to make it to the cover of Vogue magazine. But just now I noticed something in Alice's suitcase that definitely didn't belong there, "Are those two furry ears?" Immediately Alice flipped my bunny's ears over, and hid him under a towel, "No." Of course it was my bunny, ever since the first day here at university she would love to steal it from me. But it was my Bunny! I had shot it myself at a booth at the fair. With my first rifle; Dad had bought it for me not a quarter of an hour before. The owner of the booth was not very happy, but I had a talent for shooting. And since my parents got divorced not even half a year later, my Bunny accompanied me everywhere since then. Alice looked at me in her romper suit, and begged. What was also such a peculiarity of hers: Her whimsical nightwear. Sexy were these extremely wide things with a cut like a star not, especially not in baby-pink. But incredibly comfortable! Okay, I preferred my ankle-length nightgowns. But Alice was into these things. She had eight of them, numbered consecutively. Seriously. In the back, at the level of her left buttock, there was a unicorn with a number on each one. From one to eight. I'm not kidding. Anyway, she looked at me with a heartwarming pout, then got my Bunny out of her suitcase again anyway, and whispered in his long, left ear, "Maybe next time, okay?" "This is never going to work," I grumbled a bit as Alice took Bunny back to his usual spot on our sofa. "Yes, it will," she grumbled protesting, "one day I'm going to kidnap it." "Then I'll send the cops on you," I predicted nastily in response. already Alice was bracing her left arm on her hip, half-turning to face me, and was grinning at me in a sugary sweet voice, "You wouldn't." True, I wouldn't. But now, that was mostly because of the look she just gave me. The one she had already given me a few times. And which had also already led to success. The first time I just remembered already again ... We were invited to a party, and drove there in my car at eight o'clock. We also left around eight, only the following morning. Alice was clearer in her head than I was, so I let her drive. I realized that she was just as drunk as I was when we found ourselves in the middle of a dirt road with an empty gas tank. I had meanwhile slept a little in the car, and was therefore completely surprised. But there came her look, just like the one I had just seen. I could not be angry with her. Alice was a little sad about her mishap with the empty tank, so I gave her a kiss. Actually, just to comfort her. But then, she started to comfort me! Afterwards, I was a little embarrassed, because I had, so to speak, seduced Alice into this lesbian philandering. But during our subsequent search for a gas station, it quickly became clear that there was nothing to be embarrassed of. Even though it had previously seemed that Alice couldn't live without guys, she was partial into both. Which was to take its revenge once again. A few weeks later, I would have found myself a real hottie. Lisa something, I've already forgotten her last name. Anyway, we had arranged to meet for dinner; so, I got dressed up, and went out. Unfortunately, I had arrived at the restaurant too early, and had actually to witness Alice getting out of Lisa's car in front of the restaurant! I went to Lisa and gave her a smack in the face at the middle of the street; one may could still hear the clapping in Japan. And I didn't speak a single word to Alice until the next day. But at lunch, I was allowed to learn from the girl next to me at the table that Lisa had only exploited me to get to Alice. Who was then promptly dumped by her. I immediately jumped up, and later got a warning from the principal because I was running through the lecture hall like a madwoman, where Alice actually had a lecture. But she wasn't there, I found her in our room in the quad. Packing. We talked and cried for three hours. After that we apologized to each other and everything was fine again. Well, and since then there is something going on with Alice from time to time. We are not a couple or something, we still go out and have fun with others. Sometimes, I am a little bit jealous, but that is very rare. With Alice it's more of a casual thing. Okay, except for that one time. She wanted to watch a movie, but it was out of Prime and cost three dollars again. I just jokingly said that I would give her the money if she ... Well, nevermind. Anyway, the three dollars was really well spent. So, while I was grinning and reminiscing, and Alice was clearly sticking her butt out at me because of my grin, her phone rang. Already by the ringtone I recognized who was calling: her aunt. That was also something to wonder about Alice. For as long as I had known her, she went to visit her aunt once a month for the weekend. Her aunt had to live nearby, but I didn't know her name, nor did I know the address. Alice made a huge secret of it, never giving away even a tiny bit. She just went to her aunt's house and that was it. Basically, it was none of my business, but someday I would find out. Anyway, she disappeared into the bathroom with her phone, I rolled back to my desk and closed my term paper.

Four hours later, I was way too early, but already had the highway behind me, the country road under my wheels, and was on my way to my job: house sitting. With a regular customer, Mrs. Garcia. She drove every half year overnight to visit her daughter in the neighboring town, but didn't want to leave her house unattended during that. Yes, there are some strange people. But such people finance my studies. Besides, I always looked forward to seeing Mrs. Garcia, because it wasn't really about her residence. It was about the huge greenhouse behind it. Because, Misses Garcia grew orchids, and I took great pleasure in spending the night in that nasally, tropically hot back-of-house jungle. Even though I didn't have to, because everything in there was automatic. Still, I would sleep there, and because of the incredible heat, I never needed a nightgown when I slept over before. Or a comforter. Or a bed at all. I usually lay on the floor on a thin sleeping pad and sucked the scent of the flowers deep into me. However, I already suspected that it would not come to that this time, when the glass dome roof came into view. For there was a car at the entrance to the property, with a tow truck in front, and Misses Garcia behind it, and another woman I didn't know. I slammed on the brakes, pulled over, and got out, "Hello Misses Garcia! Are you okay?" "Hello, Shannon!", my client waved at me kindly, "Yes, everything is fine. I was going to call you and see if maybe you could be here a little earlier. But that's all taken care of now, huh?" I was with her by now, and we hugged warmly, then she introduced me to the other woman, "This is Edna Bradshaw, she lives right around here. Her car broke down. Right in front of my driveway, figure that out." "Well, you're in luck, Mrs. Bradshaw," I said politely, handing her my gawking eyes. My hand! I reached out my hand to her! "Oh well," waved off Misses Garcia, "to have my son-in-law Teddy, of all people, come to get the car, that's what I call luck." Misses Bradshaw accepted my hand, "Yes, you have a point. After all, Tony's Towing Service doesn't run without your son-in-law, they'd be out of business by now. Hello Shannon. And please, Edna. 'Mrs. Bradshaw' makes me feel old."

She certainly didn't look like it. Well, that old. Older than me, yes. She was much taller, stronger, and a bit plump. That's why I got big eyes, because everything about her was fuller. Everything! I had definitely noticed the slightly arrogant undertone regarding Mrs. Garcia's son-in-law, had to smile promptly and returned in kind, "Yes, Tony would be lost without him." "Told you so," Misses Garcia acknowledged herself, patting her son-in-law on the back. Mrs. Bradshaw, however, let go of my hand a little too late. I noticed, looked to her, and was she glaring at me right now!? No, I'm sure she wasn't. Or was she? "Oh, I haven't told you yet, Shannon," Mrs. Garcia turned to me apologetically, "I'm really sorry. But I guess Mrs. Bradshaw here will have to stay the night with you. Teddy can't possibly fix her car today, so he's going to take me right over to my daughter's and Edna will stay here with you. I hope you don't mind." The last wasn't a question, but an announcement. Nevertheless, I went for it, "Of course not, Mrs. Garcia. You're the boss. We'll get along just fine. Won't we?" "Sure we will," Edna nodded. I had emphasized my last question very clearly, but there was no twinkle in Edna's answer this time. Probably I had simply been mistaken. "All right, I'm ready," Teddy announced, Mrs. Garcia just getting into the tow truck. He shook his head briefly, and said, "I'm really sorry, Edna. But you know her for what she is." "Be glad you only have her on your back once every six months," came back kindly and understandingly, "and get out of here already. We'll be all right here. And say hello to Karen!" Teddy was already on his way forward at the last sentence. He waved again, then got in, leaving Edna and me behind.

And a suitcase. Edna noticed the look on my face, "Oh yes, it's mine. I've been on the road, and tonight I think I'll need something else out of it." 'I guess I will,' I thought to myself, because I didn't had anything else with me. But I said, "Oh, that's no problem. We'll just put that in the trunk, and then we'll drive down to the house. Shall we?" Edna nodded with a smile, and there was the sparkle again. Or was it? Deception or not, there was only one way to find out. I grabbed the suitcase, Edna did too, and together we dragged it across the dusty hard shoulder to my car. Loaded up quickly, Edna and I got in, too, and drove along what was still a half-mile to the house. "So, glad to be home again?", I inquired politely, but it was nothing more than small talk. Sure, everyone is glad to arrive home after a long trip. But Edna stated, "No, I wasn't that far away. I was just visiting relatives, too, like Luanda." "A daughter too?", I wanted to know, Edna shook her head, "No, my brother. He's almost ten years older than me and has some problems. But he's getting it together." That was my cue to change the subject. No one wants to listen to strangers who whine about their family, "Sure he will. Let's hope Mrs. Garcia left us something in the fridge. Because I'm hungry." "For sure," said Edna, "and if not, we'll raid all the cupboards and make whatever we feel like!" 'I'd think of something,' I thought, squinting at the stretching top on the passenger seat, only it had nothing to do with food. Only seconds later we had arrived, I stopped, and we got out. We had Edna's suitcase out of the trunk quickly too, as well as my backpack. "So little?2 wondered Edna, I swallowed my thoughts and calmly said, "It's only for one night.2 There really wasn't more in there than the folded up sleeping pad, a pair of briefs, a nightgown just in case, and my Bunny. Understanding, Edna wiggled her head, and I followed her in. We went our separate ways until dinner, with Edna's path really only leading to the phone, the bathroom, and then the sofa. Me, on the other hand, made my way to the greenhouse, and wallowed in the intangible scents. Unfortunately, dressed; but at least I was here. For dinner we had agreed on frozen pizza, and so we met again by the stove in the kitchen. Edna had meanwhile squeezed into a very comfortable-looking house dress, with the plunging neckline revealing more than was actually necessary to see. I liked it, of course, but I was really hungry now. I would probably take care of the other tonight in bed. So, we ate, talking nicely and artfully, the pizza. I was just shoving my last bite into my mouth when - I noticed wet spots on Edna's breasts. Right there. Which Edna noticed and apologized, "Oh dear, I'm sorry about that now. It's never stopped since I had my son back then." Immediately she got up, went to the cupboard, and took out a roll of kitchen towels. I stared at her breasts, unable to continue eating. I wasn't disgusted or anything. On the contrary, I was fascinated! Edna stopped at the cupboard, turned to me, and looked me straight in the eye. And there it was, the sparkle. Definite, undeniable, and very obvious. Almost prancing, she came back to the table, leaned way over, and handed me the paper towel, "Do you want to take care of ... the problem?" I reached for the paper towels and just nodded. Stiff with awe, I watched silently as Edna widened the neckline of her dress, and held her plump breasts out to me. Only the hem held them back now, but with my gentle help, both were quickly freed. Carefully, I rubbed them, but they didn't stop dripping. "Hmm," Edna sighed and swayed her upper body gently back and forth, "I guess it won't work like that, huh? Shall we try something else?" Without being able to take my eyes off the swaying in front of me I just nodded, already Edna was stroking my head lovingly and then lifted my face towards hers, "Well, lay down on the table in the living room, will you? And don't fall off." She gave me another kiss on my hair and I left. In the living room I first removed three chairs from the heavy oak table, they would only disturb anyway. Then I crawled up and lay down on my stomach. A warm, joyful expectation spread through me. Never before had I slept with someone who had to be clearly more experienced than I was. And was so ... powerful. Not in terms of actual power, but in terms of her fullness. Edna wasn't fat, though! There was just enough on her to touch, and also to squeeze and cuddle and play with ... Footsteps came closer, I did not look. With my eyes closed, I expected the unexpected. Which did happen. A bag was placed in front of me and Edna stroked my back with index finger from neck to buttocks. With an incredibly warm and loving voice she said, "But my sweet darling can't stay like that, huh? I can't reach anything?" Smiling, I was just about to straighten up a bit and then turn around, when Edna grabbed, hold and heaved my body around in one piece. With only two grips that had probably been practiced for a long time, she managed to turn me from my prone position onto my back without any problems. Now I was impressed! This would certainly be very interesting. With a sweet smile, she briefly played with my nose, then pulled and pushed me a little on the table. I returned the smile. But strangely enough, not because I wanted to. It just happened that way. For no particular reason, I grinned to myself like a baby and had no idea why. Simply because I was being smiled at. Edna tickled me on the belly, quite automatically I tightened myself giggling, bent only very slightly the legs thereby, and already my trousers went down to my knees. "Hush-hush!" went Edna, I had to laugh, and the pants fell all the way to the floor. Even as I laughed, Edna lifted me by the scruff of the neck and pulled my blouse over my head with no problem. With a startled look on her face, she showed it to me, then my top also landed where the pants already were. Held with my left arm and released by a perfect grip, my bra now disappeared as well. I was laid back on the table, my panties were grabbed at the hips and pulled over my butt. I wanted to help and join in, but that wasn't necessary at all. As if she had done this a thousand times before, Edna lifted my legs, and I was naked; my socks had disappeared into the panties together. All this happened in such a short time that I couldn't really believe it. But I also didn't want to. For an incomprehensible reason I just let happen what was done to me. And I felt great about it! So content and safe and cared for and protected, it was just wonderful. Again, Edna tickled me, pressed her mouth on my belly and then blew air hard through her lips. Again, I had to laugh, Edna repeated her game. But then I got big eyes, because by the tickling and laughing I just realized that I should actually before what would probably happen, better go to the toilet again. This was probably the moment Edna had been waiting for. She pulled me by

44

the hips a bit to her, so that my knees now hung over the edge of the table. Already she bent over me, pulled the bag from before to herself, opened it and took out - a diaper!? She put it next to me, then added wet wipes and baby powder. Noticing my incredulous questioning look, Edna said very sweetly, "Well you can't walk around naked all day, sweetie." I couldn't? Okay, whatever. Wondering at myself, I artfully shook my head. What the heck was I doing? Without grumbling or protesting, I let Edna wipe me clean with my legs now bent and spread wide. A little powder to the right places, then legs together again and with my feet supported on Edna's bosom, I dutifully lifted my butt. Already the diaper was placed, my legs wide again and after only a few moves it was sitting in its place. And I just let it happen. Without thinking about it, as if that were completely normal and should not be different. I even felt really good about it! Extremely well, as if I had waited for years only for it, and now finally it would happen. Also, my desire for Edna was not influenced by what she was doing to me. On the contrary I could hardly wait what would happen next! But for Edna it was probably not different, because she bent over me again, and gave me a kiss that I lost my mind. Her soft and still wet breasts weighed heavily on me and I enjoyed it. Right now, I could hardly imagine anything more beautiful. From her bag, still above me, she pulled out a little shirt and wiped her breasts with it. Then she lifted my upper body, sat me up and pulled it over me. Another reach into the bag was followed by a soft brush and two hair ties, and only a few minutes later I had a braid each on the right and left side of my head. "Now you're a fine sweetheart, aren't you?"

teased Edna me, I nodded weightily and almost instinctively reached out my arms to her. Without hesitation she reacted, grabbed, lifted me up and carried me pressed against her belly seemingly without much effort to the sofa. There she let herself fall with me and a "Huiiii!" to the cushions. I giggled and thought it was great! Immediately after that I was tickled through, covered all over with loving kisses and gently stroked at the same time. I liked it more and more, but then I had to catch my breath. Edna recognized my need for a break. This time I had to join in a little, but then I lay in the most comfortable pose and held by her on Edna's lap. With my head lying in the crook of her arm, her bare breasts still hanging out of her dress against my cheek and her right hand on my butt; it was just wonderful. My fingers knew nothing else to do but reach for her breasts and gently knead them. The drops became more, I could not escape this sight. Edna saw it and let me sink down a little in her arms. The grip around my shoulders tightened a little, her right hand left my butt and gently placed my playing hands on my belly. Then she stroked her chest, played briefly with the areolas before my eyes, then grabbed and held her left breast in front of my mouth. With the now clearly protruding nipple she played around my lips, promptly I automatically opened my mouth. Edna already sank her breast into it, I enclosed it tightly with my lips, and began to suck. Warm, slightly greasy and a little salty, the fine streams from Edna's breast ran over my tongue, my body relaxed noticeably, and a downright tingling bliss arose in me that I had never experienced before. Edna only intensified my feelings by gently penetrating my diaper with her right hand, and massaging my mons veneris with a light squeeze. The moving skin of my labia rubbed thereby very easily at the right place. Stimulated by all this, gentle waves ran through me, spreading more and more. What I ignored was the pressure in my bladder, stimulated by the massage. Soon, I could hardly tell the two apart, I rose higher and higher in waves - and then it happened. With an almost explosive feeling, my mind became billions of sparks, I almost sucked Edna's breast in, and wetted my diaper at the same time. My womb became hot and heavy, my mouth flooded with Edna's milk, and a deep, ecstatic growl left my throat through my nose. I shivered, froze, and sweated at the same time, my vision blurred, and all the bliss in the world blossomed throughout my body. Colors, sounds and wild shapes swam before my eyes, I could hardly catch my breath, and now burst into a thousand individual parts! As if stuck in a shell, I experienced for seconds a previously unknown world in which nothing was impossible! But nothing lasts forever, and so I also returned again to the reality. But it had changed by the things I just gone through. It played no more role to me how it was before. In the reverberation of my happiness, memories that had long been suppressed suddenly reappeared in my head. The embarrassing rejection of my first girlfriend when I wanted to be cradled by her like a baby. The one-time stealing of a pacifier in the supermarket, only to fall asleep peacefully with it in the evening. My actual envy of Alice's so unspeakably cute nightwear. Our sometimes so intimate moments, which had nothing at all to do with sex: gentle stroking, soft holding, quiet humming, and the resulting

peacefulness. I was happy. Now. In this very moment. That was all I could expect from life. Except that maybe someone would change my diaper. Because even though the warm, wet feeling was wonderful at first, this thing printed with lots of little flowers and little elephants was starting to get uncomfortable. Edna noticed my slight squirming and soft humming, she immediately responded, "What's wrong with my sweetheart, huh? Did you wet yourself or something?" Examining the outside of the diaper she pressed, and found out, "All full! Such a good girl. Well, let's fix that, shall we?" She sat me up carefully, but held me tightly and rose. Still holding me, Edna sank to one knee in front of me, grabbed me and lifted me up. Pressing me to her side and wrapping both arms around her neck, she carried me to the table. But she did not set me down as I had assumed. Edna just grabbed the bag, now holding it and me with her strong arms, and she was already carrying me upstairs to the bedroom. Similar to how she had lifted me off the couch, she now lowered me onto the bedspread, set the bag down, and laid me on my back. With a few grips, she pushed me into the middle of the bed, took off first her dress, and then my diaper. The wet wipes treatment followed, only this time gentler, and more thorough. The powder stayed off, and covering me with kisses, Edna lay down on top of me, "Well, did you like that?" "Yes," I nodded, "insanely." "Do you still want Mommy to help you fall asleep?" she asked, beginning to rub against me. How could I have said no? So, I nodded again, already Edna was reaching under my back and rolling us both around. My legs were still wide from cleaning, Edna now opened hers and placed me where she
48

wanted me. A little bit we slid up to the headboard, then Edna leaned back a little and pushed her pelvis forward at the same time. As I now sat between her thighs with my legs wide apart and her feet pressed me against them, her center almost engulfed mine. Gently Edna now moved her pelvis up and down, while at the same time holding me under the armpits only slightly lifted and lowered again. To move myself was not possible, I was completely dependent on Edna. Her movements became firmer, my breathing deeper and my gaze fixed only on her face. Her eyes spied my every movement, every sound, and every breath. But this time she was not the caregiver, not the loving mommy. Now it was her turn, I was her means to an end. And I begrudged her! My facial expression became more demanding, she understood me and intensified her efforts. My arms found her knees, Edna's hands now embraced my breasts and leaning on her I took control. Fiercely, I ran my lap over hers, slowly Edna stiffened and I sped up a little. She left my body and now supported herself on her forearms, came closer with her upper body and I grabbed her nipples. Strongly kneading and pulling I held on to them, Edna's response came immediately! With a sharp cry she acknowledged my grips, I intensified my movements and Edna collapsed jerking wildly. She tried to close her legs, but she only pushed me closer to her. She couldn't lift me away; she had no choice but to rebel and wrap her arms around me. I pushed a few more times until Edna agonizedly made me understand that she could take nothing more. Only now I let up, freed myself from the still tight grip of her thighs and fell together with her on the bed. Panting, Edna gasped tremulously, I embraced and stroked her. Slowly she regained her breath, her happy face made me feel content too, and I just pulled the covers over us.

"Good morning," someone purred softly in my ear. My face was covered with soft kisses, then my neck and breasts. Slowly the comforter disappeared towards my feet, a mouth kissing me followed. Excited, I growled, but turned onto my stomach. It helped nothing, the blanket was gone and my ass was groped. Gently but forcefully hands went between my legs, pushed them apart and lifted my hips. Without difficulty Edna found space between my knees. She deeply pressed my face into the pillow, deeply pressed Edna her face into my lap from behind. "This is how I want to be woken up every day from now on," I said delightedly, Edna extended her tongue and began. It didn't take her long, pleasant warmth flooded me, and I called her name loudly into the pillow. Edna tickled me, eased my hips back onto the sheet and scrambled out of bed. "You can have it," she purred against my ear again, "but my sweetie has to get up now to do it. Because Luanda has already left and ..." Immediately I snapped, "Really now!? We still have to clean up and tidy up!" Edna gently slowed me down and hugged me to her, "Well what do you think Mommy's already done, huh? My sweetie just needs to get dressed." She gave me a kiss, then sat me back on the bed, "Or do you want Mommy to help you?" Artfully I nodded, and Edna did. Deftly and quickly I was dressed, combed and the bed was made too. Then Edna grabbed me and carried me down the stairs. She set me down on the kitchen table, stowed her bag in the suitcase, and just as she closed it, the front door cracked.

I quickly slid off the tabletop and there was Mrs. Garcia standing inside, "Good afternoon! Good day! Well, that was quite a visit! Everyone was there, even neighbors I didn't even know! How are my flowers?" I didn't know! But Edna remarked, "How do you think your flowers are doing with someone taking care of them for almost twenty-four hours? Great, of course!" "Yes," I nodded studiously, "no problems at all." "Well then, all is good," Misses Garcia babbled on, "and the main thing is that my little flowers are fine. Here, Shannon, this is for you." Already casually, she held out a crumpled and speckled fifty-dollar note to me as she passed. "Oh, and Edna," she prattled on, "why did you have your car brought right over to your house? Well, I can't drive you, I'm all beat up." "I'll do that, Mrs. Garcia," I announced, reaching for Edna's suitcase. "Well then, that's fine," came from Mrs. Garcia, then she was already walking up the stairs, "I have to rest now." Without a farewell greeting, Edna and I left the house; apparently, we were both used to it. Without another word, I heaved Edna's luggage into the trunk, we got in, and slowly drove off. As soon as I could be sure that Misses Garcia couldn't see it, I leaned over to Edna and snuggled into her bosom, "Can I stay with Mommy a little longer?" "Sure you can, sweetie. Told you so," came back along with a kiss on my head, I sat back down neatly and drove the few miles to Edna's house per her instructions. It was a pretty little house, set in a slight hollow in the middle of flowering meadows. A solid, high fence with double gates enclosed everything, only the code Edna had entered gave access. It was completely safe here, no one could see what was going on. I stopped in front of the huge garage; Edna told me to get out and this time she took her suitcase herself. Making my way over the crunching gravel to the house, I still grabbed it and helped. At the front door, Edna stopped, and looked at me very sweetly, "Well, honey, here we are. You may do whatever you want here. And for as long as you want, too. There's only one little thing I've been keeping from you ..." I was a little startled, which Edna could see. Immediately she put down her suitcase and took me in her arms, "Oh don't worry, my darling. There's nothing for you to worry about, quite the opposite. You will have a wonderful time here with me - together with your little sister ..." Just at that moment, the front door opened, my jaw dropped to the floor, and a voice I knew very well called, "Bunny!!!"

Green isn't your color

There was a nervous knock on my office door, without turning away from the window I called out, "Come in!" Already the door sprang open and Steven, one of my subordinates, spoke clearly directed towards the ceiling and as usual without period: "I know I'm not supposed to disturb when the blinds are down but the Baldy wants to see you because Brexby actually sold his share as you predicted I'm already gone." The door clanged shut again and I relaxed. True, my screens on the desk had been specially placed so that no one could see me behind them; even more so when the blinds were down. Still, I had to be careful that no one caught me. Steven was very discreet, though; even if he saw something, he would keep quiet. That's why he was the only one I had allowed to come in anyway. Because all the others who had dared were now unemployed. Of course, I had fired them, no question about it. There was an additional agreement in her employment contract: Anyone who disturbs me will be fired. However, that was not in every employment contract, only for the employees over whom I ruled. That was the deal I made with Ernie when he offered me my own team after my first billion-dollar success. Of course, I was never allowed to call my boss, for whom I was now to compete, by his first name. Then even I would find a cardboard box on my desk. Has happened to many here at Exem, Bloom & Holloway; the sleaziest stock market speculators in all of New York City. For whom I worked as an analyst for five years. By choice. Because nowhere else could you get such benefits, earn so much money, and do anything and everything in your private life - the guys from "The Wolf of Wallstreet" were choirboys unlike us! But now I straightened my skirt, stood up and went to my boss. "Sit down," said Mister Ernest Bloom, after I had knocked politely on the open door, "and take a look at this. I want to put fifty in it." I skimmed the dossier of a small start-up company, "Up or down?" "Down. These fine idiots go out tomorrow morning, priced high. Sixty-four, one." I just nodded, "How much?" "A hundred at least. See that it's more." No sooner said I left, that's all I needed to know. On my way to the conference room, I walked past Karen's desk and laid the papers out for her, "Seven times in five minutes." She jumped up, and disappeared to the copier while I continued on my way. Arriving at said conference room, my team was just trundling in, much earlier than necessary. Karen wasn't back from the copier yet, after all; but this gave me a good idea of the state of the team. Barbara, the best burglar in the world. Fourteen charges, never convicted. Looked composed, so she didn't have anything going on right now. She provided me with information that couldn't be bought anywhere. Steven, he talked like a waterfall. The only time he was silent was when he was embellishing the last hours of an elderly man's life. Or he was nipping at the heels of other investors. Trudy, arrested by the FBI at sixteen for hacking the CIA via livestream. But no charges were filed because the images were not admitted by the court: Her boyfriend at the time was also seen on them, and both were somewhat busy. From her came all the data that the Internet gave - voluntarily or not. And of course, Rosemarie. Looked so harmless and yet was the most skilled pickpocket ever. She was never charged with anything, because she always got involved with a local policeman before her tours. As I looked around the room, my eyes caught my own reflection in the glass door. Admittedly, I was not a blank slate either. After elementary school, I went straight to high school, and at fourteen, college. Yale, Berkeley, MIT, Harvard - I had attended all the elite universities. And I was always kicked out in the second semester. Always for the same reason: public nuisance. I always hated having to wear clothes ...   It was only here in New York, at Columbia, that I graduated. Sophomore year, too. Then somehow, I got to Ernie, and I've been working for him ever since. I had my first million in my account after just one year, and after that, there were no limits. Porsche Panamera, the little house in Palisades, bonuses for my employees - Ernie paid for everything. As my bonus, so to speak. None of this was allowed to attract attention. It still can't. Because what we do here is not morally legal. A customer gives us money and we invest it in his name. At the same time, we bet on the stock market against the investment made, but in our name. The investment is lost, of course, and we collect a multiple of the betting proceeds. The complaining customer gets his money back - a thousand times cleaner than he gave it to us. Now

Karen came in with the paperwork, handed it to all, and walked out. My team hadn't even sat down, what was the point. They took the papers, I announced, "The old man wants to give fifty and get a hundred out. I want a hundred and eighty out, maybe two hundred. Think about it until tomorrow. Steven? Coffee: white, lots of sugar." Already everyone was disappearing and there was nothing left for me either but to slink off to my undeserved closing time and let my team work in peace. If these so-called idiots were planning their IPO tomorrow, Friday, then I would have the whole weekend to make up my mind from the data collected by my team. Ten minutes later, on my way to the elevator, I got my coffee in my hand; down in the parking garage, I dumped the vending machine liquor for good. Because, the coffee itself was not interesting, it was about the cardboard strip. The one with the nice handle so you don't burn your fingers. Everyone in the team knew the private preferences of the others; openly giving information about such things was a condition of employment for me. I didn't need envy, resentment or even rivalry in my job. So, everyone stayed nicely in his niche, and everything was fine. Sometimes we could even help each other. Like Steven had just helped me. Because between the cup and the cardboard handle were the dates for my upcoming date: Sarah, FF, E23-C-Mad, 2x. Which meant something like, Sarah likes women and is waiting at East 23rd Street and Madison Avenue for you to honk twice. I now had a day and a half to indulge my vice up in Palisades. The old house alone had cost over a million, the remodel another three. It was a simple steel lattice construction, only the front of the former house was still standing. So that the neighbors from the street couldn't get a heart attack. At the back there was only glass. Like in a greenhouse, on all sides. There was also just one big room, not a single wall, and everything, really everything, was glass. Every part on every piece of furniture that was otherwise made of wood or plastic was glass. Only the upholstery, mattress, pillows, and bedspread were made of white fabric, some important parts chrome-plated steel. The shower was free standing in the room, the bed right by the window. Only the toilet, which was also glass, was surrounded by glass walls that could be made electrically opaque. If one wanted to do so. There were no hanging lamps either: all the lighting was LED strips attached to the thin steel struts of the overall structure. Thus, nothing interfered with the view out or in. After all, that was the point; I wanted to be able to be seen, in all my glory. Just not by everyone, which also cost quite a bit of money. Every year. Because on Google Maps or Earth, instead of the house, one only saw woods - nothing is free. But as much as I was looking forward to my game: now it was time to find my guest star. It took me almost an hour to get from the office garage through the urban jungle, wait for the traffic lights to change on 23rd street, and get to the right place when the light turned red. I honked the horn twice and was greeted by ... well, hello! She was cute. A bit smaller than me, well-groomed appearance, poison-green highlights in blond hair, tight leather pants, flat shoes, jeans jacket. She opened the passenger door, hopped in, and immediately buckled her seat belt. Only then did she extend her hand to me, "Sarah. I hope you're Adele?" "Thankfully yes," I grinned at her and took her hand, "Have you been told how it goes?" "Yes. You can go back over it if you want, though. Maybe I do want to get off at the next intersection," Sarah said, eyeing me up and down. The fact that she was holding my hand made me like her. "Okay," I said, the light turned green and I started talking, "First of all you get 5000 dollars for the action and you don't have any expenses. You're free to go anytime, really anytime day or night, the cab home is on me. The conditions are simple: no touching, no sex, no hair. Do you think you can handle that?" "I need a haircut anyway," Sarah spoke up, now letting go of my hand, "now there's just one question: who's the client?" Hadn't she been told that? Looking stubbornly straight ahead, I just smiled, Sarah misunderstood me, "All right, I'll shut up already. It's none of my business." But she didn't, so shut up. No one else ever talked to me so openly. She spoke freely about her life. Her parents' house wasn't that great, school was shit, and apart from what she was doing now, she didn't have a real job. But the money would be enough, she would also be healthy and what should happen if you only choose the rich. I knew this kind of resume from somewhere, mine was not much different from hers. Except for the job, of course. Sarah seemed fun-loving, cheerful, and carefree, there seemed to be nothing she was afraid of or worried about. Again, very likeable, I thought. But that could just be acting, as with most of the girls I've had so far. Afterwards, they were usually in a completely different mood. As thought, we arrived after barely forty minutes, I stopped in front of the facade. "Fancy place," Sarah muttered, wanting to know, "Lots of bedrooms?" "Only one," I stated correctly, "but you'll see." "Then I guess I'd better not ask," she grinned and got out. I followed her, locked the car, and opened the front door for her, "Go right in! Welcome to Crystal Palace." With raised eyebrows, Sarah strode across the threshold and I walked right behind her, locking the front door behind us as well. "A little dark, huh?" asked Sarah, I had to agree with her and flipped the light switch, "Better this way?" "Looks bigger from the outside," she commented on what she could see, "is that just a closet?" "Yes, it is," I smiled nicely, "and it's there to be used. I'm going to go inside. See you in a bit." Normally, I would be the first to use the closet myself, peeling anything off my body that was constricting. "Don't think any of the clothes in here fit me!" shouted Sarah to me as I tried to walk through the door covered on the side. So, I stopped, turned to her, and said very sweetly, "You're not supposed to wear any of that stuff, sweetie." The reaction that could now be observed in her was something I had never seen before. Each of the other girls looked startled, or at least questioning. Sarah just raised an eyebrow with a grin and started to take off her jacket. Barely inside, I had little time. I quickly got rid of my skirt, blouse, stockings, and shoes. Except for two weeks in every six months, I never wore anything else. My gynecologist said that I should allow my period at least twice a year. And then just wore panties, otherwise never. I quickly pulled one of the bar stools to me, planted myself on it, and waited for Sarah. Just in time I sat down the door opened, and she appeared as God created her. Flat belly, slightly protruding hips, she also had a real butt. Nice thighs, slender legs, and feet. Her slightly hanging, but still quite neatly shaped breasts I liked very much, the grass-green hair less. But I would change that already. She entered with an interested look, eyed the part of the house she had just left and spoke, "Wow. It's damn warm in here, I wouldn't have expected that." She closed the door and now looked at me, "Wow. And neither is this." I just raised my shoulders apologetically for a moment, she immediately understood, "You're my customer, right?" "Looks like it," I said warmly, Sarah continued walking, inspecting the room and me, "Nice. And all so open." "Hmm," I just went on, "I like it that way." "Oh, just don't worry, I do too," was her nice reply. I didn't move as she circled first me and then the room, "And really no touching?" "No need," I informed her, "I'll take care of that myself." "Mhm," Sarah nodded and then audibly sat down on the sofa, "I'm curious about that." "Are you?", I asked coquettishly, getting down from the bar stool. Sarah slid forward a bit on the couch, opened her thighs with both hands, and grinned, "Can totally picture it. What is it?" Because now I had to grin too, because, "Green really isn't your color, pumpkin." "You can change anything these days," came succinctly, I already knew how, "Come here. Sit down." Pushing the bar stool in her direction, I walked towards her, Sarah stood up and then made herself comfortable on the furniture, "You can't do that without touching it, can you? Because I can't do it myself." "You don't have to," I returned sweetly, "after all, the touching thing only applies to you." "I like that better," Sarah said, shifting a little more on the stool, "would have been a bit boring otherwise." "Never a dull moment with me," I said meaningfully and walked over to the vanity. Sarah grumbled with interest, and I got the razor, leather straps, brush, soap, a towel, and two small bowls from the drawer. "So old-fashioned?", Sarah wanted to know, while I put hot water into one of the bowls, my explanation was plausible, "Removing hair painlessly is only possible this way. Electric or disposable is not thorough enough." She probably saw that, and kept silent while she continued to observe what I was doing. I put both bowls down in front of the stool, scraped a few flakes of soap into the empty bowl with the back of the knife made for this purpose, and added a few drops of water from the other bowl. With the soft brush, I began to combine everything, a few more drops and the necessary foam was already emerging. Sarah watched me with interest as I stirred vigorously and increased the amount drop by drop. Then I was ready, Sarah took a deep breath and I began to soap her against the natural direction of growth. Her neatness, which I had already noticed when she got into the car, was now clearly apparent. For if it had not been so, the foam would not remain stable. But it did, I gently massaged it in with the brush. Which already led to a reaction, because in the middle of the foam crown I applied, the tiny bubbles began to disintegrate. What also provided a warm feeling in my belly, and surprised me a little. I usually didn't have that with the other girls. But for now, I took care of Sarah's jungle and after sharpening the knife, I began delicately with the timber work. Stroke by stroke I drew the blade over her skin, stroke by stroke Sarah's breathing became deeper. After barely ten minutes, the forest had completely disappeared, and wasteland remained. With a tip moistened in the water bath I removed the last remnants of foam, with a dry one I wiped. That this dry tip was no longer dry afterwards, surprised me again a little. Inwardly, of course, I was pleased, but I could not let that show. Clearly Sarah's breath blew out of her mouth, I stood up and folded her legs closed, "So we'd have the first part." "Ouch," Sarah smiled at me. It was obvious from her face that she was struggling hard to keep her hands to herself. Interestingly, I was no different. But she did, albeit with difficulty, "Okay, then ... oh boy ... just do it." "It's not a chore, you can say no," I tried to inform her. But I didn't get any further than "you" because Sarah imperiously raised her right arm and said, "Do it, okay?" I nodded my thanks, then the game of soap and water drops began again. This time it took me longer, almost double the time. Then Sarah was bald, eyebrows and armpits included. With an incredulous but interested look, I pointed to the ceiling-high mirror on the wall by the entrance. Sarah slid off her stool and ran to it. Promptly, what always happened, happened. With her hands held in front of her mouth in shock, and eyes wide open, she looked in, "Holy shit!" But even now I noticed a differentiated reaction. For Sarah stroked both balds, turned to me, and grinned, "It's insanely sexy, though, isn't it?" "I know," I just said softly, then took off my wig and removed the eyebrows that were only glued on. "Oh," came from Sarah. Nothing more. But it was not a repulsive "oh", but a very interested understanding, "I should have guessed. Really sexy, honestly." She started circling me again, and I felt great about it. Of course, I always felt great when someone looked at me in that way. But with Sarah, it was different somehow. Tingling, yes. Exciting, yes. But at the same time familiar, comfortable, very pleasant. Yet without any strain, completely free, and unforced. Otherwise, I always announced what was coming next. Not with her, not with Sarah. I didn't have to say anything to her, she did it on her own. And she went even further, "Do you really want to leave it like that?" Her hand pointed to my lap, irritated, I looked. And noticed, of course, the tiny, but still visible stubbles. And already Sarah did something that I would not have expected: she indicated that I should not move. Then she sauntered over to the stove, got the meat tongs, grabbed my hand with them, and stroked my head with them, "Feel that?"

Completely out of my mind, I just nodded mutely, Sarah sat back down on the stool and I dutifully sat down on the floor in front of the small bowls still in front of her. Now I faltered for a moment. What had just happened? Had I let myself be told what to do? Doubting myself, I looked her in the face a little questioningly, Sarah just shrugged nicely, "A little equal right for all, right? Unless you like rough hands." Normally I would have stood up now and made it very nicely, yet firmly clear that I was the one in charge here. But I didn't. Why? I don't know. It just happened, there was nothing I could have done about it. So, I got up, emptied the water bowl, and refilled it with hot water. Went back, sat down in front of Sarah, and started the same procedure I had done on her. And I visibly liked it. In the truest sense of the word, because this Sarah watched me doing it. Very intensely even. Which, again, never ... really never? I had to think for a moment. Unfortunately, my hands did not understand so fast that they better didn't move. Already I held the blade wrong, and cut myself. I stopped in the middle of the movement. The cut was only tiny, barely deeper than a fingernail's thickness. For seconds I didn't move, just staring at the knife. Sarah didn't say a word either, but she looked at me fearfully with her eyes wide open. I felt no pain, so I just pulled the knife straight out of my skin. Why wasn't I bleeding? Surely, I should be bleeding? And there was nothing. There was now. Gently the edges reddened, then blood gathered in the wound and finally the first drop ran out. Only now did

I actually realize what had just happened. Cursing viciously, I jumped up and ran to the kitchen towels. Scolding myself, I tore off a few sheets and pressed them onto the now very painful wound. Now I noticed Sarah. She was standing next to me, still wide-eyed, stammering to herself, "I'm sorry ... I shouldn't have ... I mean ... I don't know what ... I'm sorry ..." Incensed, I looked at her. My head said kick out, my gut agreed, but my heart said no. I was torn, then out of my mouth came, "It's okay." Why hadn't I fired Sarah!? I was the boss! I called the shots! And if there was a thousand stubbles ... wait. Was it really that bad? It was already no longer bleeding, timidly I pulled the kitchen towel over my Venus mound. Scratchy. So, it was true. Annoyed, I threw the towel away from me, and looked at Sarah the same way. Very bashfully and with uncertainty in her eyes she said almost begging, "So, if you could make an exception? Just one. I'd like to put a Band-Aid on there. Just in case?" First, I followed her instructions, then I cut myself because of it, and now I was supposed to make an exception to the 'don't touch' rule on top of it!? It would come to that! "Okay," so I said, and - what!? Why was I speaking something other than what I thought!? And why didn't it upset me? I was just confused, but still excited. Not from the cut or the pain, definitely not. From Sarah. She was so ... different. Quite like the one who enjoyed the same things herself. At least, that's how it seemed to me now. Admittedly, I had never experienced that before. But should it really be possible? I didn't get to think any more, because Sarah had conjured up a first aid kit from somewhere and was kneeling in front of me, "I'll be careful, but this might hurt for a second." Expecting the pain, I pressed my mouth together as a precaution, but Sarah still had a little problem: "Could you ... I can't reach it that well." With her hands she showed me what I should do. So a very little bit I squatted and at the same time went up on my toes, tilted my pelvis forward and spread my legs. Mutely, Sarah's lips formed the words "Good God," then she gently fastened the patch. Without meaning to, a sigh escaped me, Sarah looked up at me, her right arm raised as if in slow motion. I wanted to go back. But behind me was the counter, I could not escape at all. Sarah's hand didn't want to reach me though, she just held her index finger just above my knees between my legs. Caught a sticky drop coming from my middle and showed it to me. Not capable of any reaction, I stared at Sarah. Already realizing what would happen now. What had to happen now. I couldn't stop it, not anymore. Maybe never again - and I was afraid of it. I didn't want anyone to determine over me! Nobody decides about me! No one! Not even ... me. Bullshit! I'm the only one who was in control of her life! No one in my family had ever made it this far! No one had ever cared about me! I could only help myself. Sarah wouldn't be able to, even though I had allowed her to touch me. This one time ... But I couldn't let that happen again, even though she was just putting her finger in her mouth with an unbelievably pleasurable expression. Looked at me, noticed my heart beating faster, and now allowed her finger to leave her mouth again. In my mind, I was desperately looking for a way out, knowing that there was none left. Like a ravenous deer, I awaited the inevitable - but Sarah simply stood up and said, "Yummy ... I'll put the box away again, shall I?" I stood back up normally, knowing nothing to say, and walked to the vanity. Halfway there, though, I stopped. Just like that. In the middle of the area. I turned around, Sarah was standing there. Quite dejected she started: "I messed it up, didn't I? I mean the mood. I'm really sorry. I didn't mean to. I should probably just go now; you don't have to ... what are you doing?" I didn't really know myself, but I walked up to Sarah. Knelt down right in front of her - and hugged her as tight as I could. "Okay," came from her, stammering in confusion, "that ... well ... I don't know ..." But when I looked up at her, she knew: "Oh, no." Oh yes, she did know! Because during the few steps away from her, a realization came over me like struck by lightning that I hadn't wanted to admit to myself before. Sarah was my match. The only person in the whole world who was like me. Begging, Sarah looked down at me, "Please don't ... please don't say it ..." But the corners of my mouth were already pointing up. "I'm only doing this for the money!", Sarah tried to whine to herself and me. I knew better. A long time ago. "Oh, come on ..." she complained, but my smile only widened. She sank down to me, "I only read my horoscope once." "What did it say?", I wanted to know now in a tender voice, and clasping her sweet bottom, Sarah told me, "Go out quietly, love is not waiting inside." "And, is it right?", I inquired, although I already saw the answer in her eyes. And I saw much more: me. How I had always hoped that among the many girls there would be this one. How disappointed I was when it didn't happen. When I was not contradicted. When I simply determined and everything just happened. Yes, of course I had my fun. But lied to myself for an eternity. Had persuaded myself that it had to be the same. And yet I knew deep inside that this was not the case. That I had only waited for this moment, this one person who ignited something in me. And that was now on fire! "Sure it was right," Sarah murmured, putting her hands to my cheeks, "those stupid things are always right. Now get up and make sure you get to bed." For the first time I pranced around my house with a whole horde of butterflies in my stomach. Knowing Sarah behind me, I gyrated my hips as I did so, which was instantly rewarded with a tender slap. I felt incredibly free around her, like never before. I didn't give a damn about the whole world right now, only here and now were important. I just wanted to be with her, to be around her. I stopped, because I realized something: My previous life had stopped. I couldn't and didn't want to go back! Never again. No more determining, no more taking advantage, no more running away. In a split second, I realized all of this and turned around. Sarah almost collided with me, stopped swaying for a moment and just opened her mouth to say something.

But I gently held it closed for her. Before she could protest, I whispered, "I've missed you, you know that? All my life." Sarah's shoulders slumped, her eyes filled, and my hand left her mouth. Already a tear was rolling down her cheek, she quickly wiped it away and wailed, "That's not true. Because I missed you." The shell around my usually hard heart broke, I softened. Took Sarah's hands and put them around my neck, "No more conditions." I wiped away a second tear with my thumb, then Sarah clung to me and I to her. Insanely content with the entire universe, we held each other tightly, not wanting to let go of each other. But Sarah now detached herself from me, just a tiny bit. With her eyes closed, she sucked in her lungs just above my skin, then, blinking dangerously, she looked me straight in the eye and breathed, "You smell so good ... I can't stand it anymore." She pressed her index finger between my breasts, "Bed, now." Guided by her finger, I walked backwards slowly, never taking my eyes off Sarah. When the back of my knees touched the mattress, I sat down and was about to swing my legs into bed when Sarah slyly announced, "Wrong way." With my feet turned toward the pillow, I lay down, Sarah squatting beside me. Blanket and pillow disappeared somewhere; Sarah gently pushed me a little further towards the foot end until my head was just resting on the edge. I could no longer see her this way, which I didn't like so much right now. But wait, above me in the reflection of the arched window I recognized her. And she recognized me. Now she sat at the head end, her legs wide open. Her hands slid slowly over every inch, looking me over the window right in the eyes. For the pane acted like a magnifying glass, making it easy for me to follow her every touch. Gently, Sarah ran her fingers over her bald skull, on to her neck and along the sides of her ribs to her hips. Just teasing, not triggering anything. But it did trigger something in me, and that even though I remained motionless. The mere idea of her touch on my skin could not be concealed from me for a long time, my knees slowly moved apart on the sheet. My arms also moved away from my body, my breathing deepened and it became cooler between my legs. Sarah saw the change and responded with more enthusiasm, below my belly button I felt comforting warmth inside me and began to find my rhythm of tensing and releasing. Sarah found her rhythm too, showing me more and more of her skills, bringing me to a threshold I was only too happy to cross. Just one more tiny moment, then wave after wave engulfed me. As suddenly as the surf had broken out, it ebbed away again. In contrast to other times, however, this time the storm remained and did not subside. Sarah continued to push herself, but it was not enough. She looked desperate, struggling with herself, and not managing what I had already managed. So, I straightened up and slid over to her. Without letting it come to an interruption, I pushed Sarah forward a bit, crawled behind her back, and let my hands caress her body for additional effect. This was too much; she writhed and began to twitch. With her mouth open, she made a sound like a dog and slid against me on the sheet. Her head slid along my body, I lifted myself up a bit and placed my center over her forehead. With greedy eyes Sarah saw it, I began to rub myself against her and the storm gained strength again. Only moments later I collapsed yelping, Sarah smiled and continued to move her skull. I couldn't escape like that though; her movements overloaded me and the spasming of my legs caused me to lose my footing and topple forward between Sarah's legs. Now I was free of the additional agony, but that did not apply to her. Landing in just the right place, I wrapped my arms around her thighs, held them open and drank Sarah in. That this was now too much for her, she gave me to understand with her hands on my ass, but I did not let up. Her legs stood up, but her knees could not come together. Squeaking, she reared up, despite the fact that I was sitting on her. I gave in, and with one last suck, Sarah burst into bliss. Very carefully and delicately I worked her knees, then I let myself roll away to the side. I had turned quickly, Sarah's hands demanded me and already I snuggled up to her. She was still trembling slightly, but my breathing could hardly calm down either. With, so to speak, her last strength, Sarah found a corner of the bedspread that had been laid aside, in a joint effort we pulled it over us, and in the last rays of the now setting sun we tried to kiss each other. But we were both too exhausted and spent. So, only a sigh was salvation enough, Sarah closed her eyes and I did the same.

In the middle of deep black night, I woke up. Whether I had my eyes closed or open made no difference. Lying half on top of me, however, I felt Sarah, each of her breaths penetrating my ear. I did not want to move, because this feeling, which I had missed for years, was too wonderful. I didn't want to lose it again. Not under any circumstances. I had to do something. Now. A little tighter, my hands gripped briefly, just to really feel the being of her body. Sarah must not have been sleeping so soundly, already she noticed my grip and pressed herself against me. "I'd have to get up," I remarked in a soft whisper now, Sarah's head lifting, "Me too. Who first?" "You go ahead," I said gently, "I need to make a quick phone call." Sarah's breath hitched for a moment, then she tentatively wanted to know, "You're ... not going to order a cab now, are you?" My hands found her cheeks despite the darkness, lifted her head to me, and I gave her a kiss, "No. I don't think so. I just think I'll' have to work in home office for just a few days ..."

www.ingramcontent.com/pod-product-compliance
Lightning Source LLC
Chambersburg PA
CBHW072037150726
47999CB00002B/961